Praise for

C000177226

'*Dolores* is a glowing, beatin
sentences manage to be both mysterious and precise,
creating a potent atmosphere that resonates beyond
its brevity'

Megan Hunter, author of *The End We Start From*

'*Dolores* reads the way a first novel should: short,
lyrical, intense, and with adventurous ambition'

Nell Zink, author of *The Wallcreeper*

'Rich, melodic and marked by a troubling sensuality, *Dolores* depicts the strange pleasures a young girl
might take in her body, and the perils and libera-
tions such pleasures hold'

Sue Rainsford, author of *Follow Me To Ground*

'*Dolores* is propulsive, atmospheric, wonderfully pe-
culiar, a little dark. A dreamy hallucination'

Amina Cain, author of *Indelicacy*

'A succinct, intense story . . . this atmospheric debut
is a deliciously satisfying read about a girl at a criti-
cal juncture in her life'   *Book Riot*

'A taut and moody novella . . . In burnished prose, Curtis raises potent questions about how women control their bodies and destinies when subject to institutional forces'

'So well written . . . By keeping the narrative tight, she's able to put care into each sentence and this pays off with a kind of warmness that encompasses the characters in its glow'   *Readings*

'Precise, intense and aching, *Dolores* moves seamlessly between sensuality and realism. I read it in a couple of fevered hours and lived in its heady atmosphere for days afterwards'

Julia Armfield, author of *Salt Slow*

'Blurring the borders past and present, sex and religion, desire and shame, a short and potent story of a young woman in trouble'   *Irish Times*

'This skilfully written and disquieting novella . . . is a hypnotic and powerfully affecting read'

Sydney Morning Herald

Lauren Aimee Curtis was born in Sydney in 1988. Her fiction and essays have appeared, or are forthcoming, in *Granta*, *The White Review*, *The Atlas Review*, *The Lifted Brow* and *Fireflies*, among other publications. Her first book, *Dolores*, was published in 2019. She has recently completed a PhD on the work of Renata Adler and Elizabeth Hardwick at the University of Technology Sydney, and is currently at work on her next book.

DOLORES

LAUREN AIMEE CURTIS

WEIDENFELD & NICOLSON

First published in Great Britain in 2019 by Weidenfeld & Nicolson
This paperback edition published in 2020 by Weidenfeld & Nicolson
an imprint of The Orion Publishing Group Ltd
Carmelite House, 50 Victoria Embankment
London EC4Y 0DZ

An Hachette UK Company

1 3 5 7 9 10 8 6 4 2

A CIP catalogue record for this book is
available from the British Library.

ISBN (Mass Market Paperback) 978 1 4746 1251 7
ISBN (eBook) 978 1 4746 1194 7

Typeset by Input Data Services Ltd, Somerset

Printed and bound in Great Britain by Clays Ltd, Elcograf S.p.A.

www.orionbooks.co.uk
www.weidenfeldandnicolson.co.uk

DOLORES

Dolores wasn't the name her mother had given her when she arrived in the world, feet first. It was what the nuns called her because she spoke Spanish, because they knew she'd made her way to the convent from another country, via Seville. *Dolores,* the nuns had said. It was a name that referred to aches and pain. Our Lady of Sorrows. Dolores was sixteen when she arrived at the convent. Her body was already awkward. Her mouth was full of crooked teeth. She did not know how to smile. When Dolores tried to smile, she looked as though she were being pinched by small, hidden hands. She climbed the mountain carrying a Bible and a small postcard of the Virgin of Macarena and she wore on her head a makeshift veil. It was, in fact, a dirty lace tablecloth she had attached to her hair with a few pins. *Dolores.*

No, it wasn't her name, but it's what she should have been called.

It was the end of June, on a forty-degree day, when

the iron gates to the convent opened and Dolores was carried in. Six months later, she was kneeling in the thick snow by those very gates, making a deal with God. Hours later, she watched from the hospital bed as the nuns crowded around the incubator, cooing and praying, hunched over what looked like a small blob of angry flesh. *Francisco*, the nuns were saying as they stroked the plastic box. *Francisco*. They had already named her son.

When does Dolores' story begin? From the first memory and then again from each variation of that same memory that comes after. Dolores was always reaching towards her past. Cold hands grasping in the dark. She was always gesturing, somewhat slyly, towards her future. If anything, her story must start somewhere in the middle.

JUNE

She stood at the bottom of a long, sloped driveway. On her right was a large wooden letter box and to her left was a marble statue of the Madonna and child. The baby had healthy rolls of fat and an old wise face. The virgin looked serene. The convent was beyond the statue, at the top of the hill. In the glare from the sun, it looked like a golden slab of sandstone. She could see a covered balcony with large arches, rows of small windows, black iron gates at the front. Nothing else around but clouds, some trees and large rocks that jutted out from the side of the mountain. Silence except for a few crows. The sun was in the middle of the sky. The air was thick and oppressive. As she began to walk up the driveway, her stomach gurgled and her head felt light. Halfway up the hill she stopped to vomit. When she reached the gates, she collapsed. Some of the nuns were outside gardening. What they saw was this: a squat-looking girl with a tablecloth pinned to her head, kneeling at the gates, then falling on her face.

There she is: *Dolores*. Newly named. Sitting at the kitchen table inside the convent, conscious of how bad she must smell. Her armpits are wet. Her mouth is dry. The nuns gather around her. Without saying a word, one of them places a glass of water in front of her. Dolores drains it quickly. The nun picks up the glass, slowly, and fills it once more. Dolores drinks. The water runs out the side of the glass and down her neck.

Later, that same nun leads Dolores to the chapel – a small room with stained-glass windows and wax on the floor. The nun takes both of her hands and holds them in her own. Her skin feels cold. Her voice is soft. At times, she slips into dialect. She motions for Dolores to kneel. Whenever the nun prays, Dolores bows her head and prays too. Whenever the nun crosses herself, Dolores crosses herself. After the nun has repeated the same phrase several times, slowly, pleadingly, and looks into her eyes, Dolores cannot help but respond by nodding solemnly. The nun is small and frail. She looks like a child in an old woman's body. She kisses

Dolores' hands. Her face cracks into a large smile.

After their conversation, the nun walks with Dolores, arm in arm, around the convent and up the stairs to a long and narrow room on the second floor. There are twelve single beds. Twelve small bedside tables. Twelve chests. She is told to sleep. One of the nuns closes the blinds. The walls are rock. The room is cool. Dolores closes her eyes.

Bells ring in the background of her dreams. When she wakes, it's the middle of the night, dark except for a slither of light on the wall from the moon. Her eyes adjust. There are sleeping bodies all around her. Some of the nuns are snoring. She studies the outlines of their bodies, the different colours of their hair. White, brown, red, speckled black and grey. She feels something heavy at the end of the bed, resting on her feet. Someone has left a pile of clothes. Long-sleeved cotton shirts and two loose smocks. One woollen jumper. Some kind of cape. A veil. Stockings, socks and underwear. She buries her nose in the clothing. It smells of mothballs, stale soap and onions. She remembers the backpack she arrived with and gets up to look for it.

Someone has placed it on the chest at the end of her bed. There are things missing – her clothes, her passport. She climbs back into bed and closes her eyes.

It's a large room that sits adjacent to a church. There are four rows of tables. Fake flowers and balloons. Standing in the corner, Dolores sticks one of her fingers into a soft sponge cake. She is twelve years old. It's her cousin's fifteenth birthday party. At her mother's insistence, Dolores wears a white taffeta dress and a red ribbon in her hair. Little gold shoes. She looks like a dessert. Like the seven-tiered cake that sits on the table to her left surrounded by smaller cakes, pink meringues, bowls of whipped cream. Dolores takes her finger out of the sponge cake and wipes it on the back of her dress. At the opposite end of the room, all of her uncles sit together at one of the tables, smoking and drinking. Their wives are standing nearby, arranging the food. Some of the other aunts are in the small kitchenette to the side, secretly smoking. At the head of an empty table, her grandmother sits alone, grimacing. The youngest cousins sit on the floor by the presents. The oldest cousins have escaped to the church basement. There is a band on the small stage, tuning their instruments. The dance floor is empty, for now.

Liliana is ten. She follows Dolores around the room. Liliana never brushes her teeth and she cries all the time. Here she is in the church hall: Liliana. She has snot on her face. She wears a matching tracksuit, eggshell blue. She truly is a child. She has a secret handshake with her mother. Standing in the corner by the cake, Dolores and Liliana talk about their cousin who has just turned fifteen. The birthday girl stands in the centre of the room in a dress that is both tight and puffy. She has small crystals on her nails and in her hair. Her lips are dark red. Her eyelids, baby blue. Her arms are bare. Around her neck, she wears a long gold chain. *She looks like a small, fat man,* Liliana says.

Paper plates are passed around. Everyone lines up to eat. During lunch, at the other end of the room, two uncles begin to yell. Someone breaks a chair. Everybody laughs. The uncles hug. The birthday girl approaches the dance floor smiling, and her father weeps loudly. The band begins. The wives clear the plates; they emerge from the shadows carrying plastic bins. They retreat to the kitchenette where they will stay for most of the evening, peeking over the swinging doors every so often.

Dolores and Liliana slip out of the room. Standing at the end of a narrow hallway at the bottom of the stairs, they press their ears against the door to the church basement.

Muffled voices and music on the other side. Some shouting. Liliana turns to face Dolores, grins, then knocks four times on the door. Loud knocks. The music stops. The door opens and the smell of smoke floods out. It smells different from the smoke upstairs. Standing at the door is their eldest cousin. Behind him, sitting on the floor, are a group of boys. Some of them are cousins but there are strangers too, and just one other girl. She sits cross-legged on a desk. The eldest cousin lets out a long sigh. His eyes are half closed. His mouth twists into a smile. *No kids,* he says, and slams the door. Liliana knocks again. *All right, all right,* he says as he opens the door, *but you have to act like adults.*

Inside the room the light is different. There are no windows. It's almost completely dark except for a single bulb that sits at the top of a tall lampstand. Part of the room is sectioned off with a faded red curtain. There are vestments hanging from nails on the walls, Bibles scattered on the floor and a large broken crucifix propped up against a filing cabinet.

The eldest cousin is holding a small flask. Dolores takes it from him and drinks, gives it to Liliana. All of the boys are shoeless. Their shirts are unbuttoned. They sit with their legs spread out on the floor. Dolores tugs at her dress. There is a boy standing next to the girl who sits on the desk. His jumper is dark green. Even from across the room, in the dark, Dolores can tell that he is looking at her. The flask goes around the circle.

We were playing a game before you arrived, one of the boys on the floor says. Someone has turned on the small stereo in the middle of the circle. *It's called . . .* and here the boy lingers on the word, rolling it on his tongue, before announcing: *Guess my underwear.* There is laughter.

The eldest cousin points to the boy with the green jumper. *Red,* he says, and the boy sighs, shakes his head and pulls his pants down. The lamp is pointed in his direction and he appears in front of the faded curtain bathed in a weak spotlight. His underwear is small and black, the kind that Dolores' father wears.

The boy smiles and turns to the girl on the table. *Nothing*, he says. Everyone laughs, including the girl, who stands up and does a half twirl as she pulls up her skirt. Her underwear is dark blue, lacy, grown-up.

The girl returns to the desk and looks at Liliana. *Disney*, she says. Everyone howls. Liliana shakes her head. A chant begins. *Show us, show us, show us*. Liliana's face is red and sweaty. The chant continues.

She doesn't wear any, Dolores says, because it's the truth. A little squeal from Liliana: *It's not true*. One of the boys on the floor turns the lamp to face her. *Prove it*, he says. The chant stops. Liliana holds the waistband of her tracksuit protectively, shakes her head. The boys slap the ground. They roll around on the floor laughing. Tears roll down their faces. Dolores knows, she can tell by the expression on Liliana's face, that she's about to cry. So she doesn't look at her. She turns to the boy on her right and laughs with him. Liliana runs out of the room, slamming the door as she goes.

The game dissolves. Dolores lingers. An hour or so more of drinking from the flask – it burns her throat, the heat travels all the way down to her stomach. Then, the older girl and the boy with the green jumper leave. The eldest cousin leaves. Everyone leaves until it's just Dolores and three strangers lying on the floor behind the red curtain. She lets them stick their fingers inside her, one by one. So this is what it feels like, she thinks. Lying there, on the floor of the church basement, she can hear the thud of bass coming from above. Offbeat stomping, drunken singing, and her aunt's long, high-pitched laugh.

Afterwards, when Dolores climbs the stairs alone, she walks into a different party. Everyone is dancing. Balloons are bursting. The eldest cousin swings his mother around the room. Liliana sits underneath the dessert table, eating cake. The birthday girl is crying in the kitchenette. Dolores' grandmother sits in exactly the same position as before, grimacing. There is a plate of food in front of her, untouched. Dolores sits beside her, picks up a cold chicken wing from the plate and sucks the meat from the bone.

Her grandmother's hands are resting on the table. Dolores places her free hand on top. She watches her mother and father dance. Their heads are resting on each other's shoulders as they move together, slowly.

JULY

JULY

The nuns never wash themselves. That's one of the first things she notices. They have yellow-green gunk in the corners of their eyes, their tongues are brownish-pink, and there are flakes of dead skin on their noses. Their breath is bad. They have wild hairs that curl at the bottom of their chins. Dolores doesn't look at the nuns directly. She keeps her head down and her eyes lowered. The only time she can look closely at their faces is during prayer in the chapel or at night while they sleep. In the mornings, the nuns kneel in the chapel, the first light enters the room, and Dolores looks around at their scrunched-up faces, deep in thought.

By now, she knows that the nun who spoke to her in dialect, inside the chapel, is the mother superior and must be obeyed. To eat something, she must ask the mother. To write a letter, drink an extra glass of water, or collect the eggs from the garden – the mother must give permission. But the mother is kind. She often gives permission with a small nod and a smile. And Dolores spends most of her time with the mother – they study the Bible together for two hours each day, sitting side by side at an old wooden desk in the study room. At the end of each session, the mother takes Dolores' hands, as she did that first day, and holds them close to her heart. She repeats certain phrases. Here are the words she most often says: *sin, hell, redemption, saved, sister.* And then: *Do you understand?* Dolores always nods solemnly, even if she doesn't.

What does the mother superior know about her? Her name, age, and place of birth. This, she must know from Dolores' passport, which the mother says she has locked in her office, for safekeeping. Everyone in the convent still calls her Dolores. So why does it sound so different in the mouth of the mother superior? When the mother superior says her name, it sounds as though it were travelling down a slide. *Do-lor-es,* the mother says, with the *es* finishing nice and low.

At the convent, among the group of nuns, there are just three who are yet to take their first vows. Three who wear the same button-up blouse and loose brown smock as Dolores. Battered leather shoes and a light-blue veil. Two are tall and one is short. One has green eyes and dimpled cheeks. One has an extra-large tooth that hangs outside of her lip. One has a large, round, and translucent face, like the moon. They are always together. They walk through the corridors of the convent in a triangular shape – one at the front and two at the back – their long smocks swishing. And when they say her name, they do so in unison, lingering on the middle syllable each time. *Do-lorrr-es,* they say.

On the rare occasion that Dolores encounters one of them alone, everything about them changes: their walk, their posture, even their voices. The beautiful one chews her nails down to stubs. Sometimes, the moon-faced one secretly smiles at Dolores. It's the hang-tooth one that she must watch. It's the hang-tooth one that she finds one night, while it's still dark and everyone is asleep, rummaging through the chest that sits at the bottom of her bed. Dolores wakes from the sound and sits up slowly. The girl is kneeling on the floor with her head inside the chest. She looks up and their eyes meet. For a moment, the hang-toothed girl looks shocked, but then her face twists into a snarl. She spits, then walks back to her bed.

Dolores pulls the covers up to her neck and watches the slither of light from the moon edge across the wall. She waits to hear the sound of the morning bells. Dolores prays. Her prayers are different to the ones she says throughout the day, in the chapel, and in unison with the other nuns. Those prayers are for the world. But alone, in bed, in the shadowy night while the other nuns sleep, Dolores can privately ask for what she wants. She knows no one else is listening. Her mother once told her that prayers are wishes. In bed, at the convent, Dolores makes private wishes. After each prayer, she preemptively thanks the Lord for granting her wish. Only then does she fall asleep.

Brown carpet. Radio clock that sits on top of the fridge. The wooden bar in the corner of the living room. At night, in the convent, between prayers and sleep, Dolores walks around the apartment she grew up in. The couch is pink. Worn and cracked leather. There are cotton pillows with embroidered edges, one with a stain from when her younger brother had a nose bleed. Scuff marks on the wall behind the door. And in the kitchen, by the phone, glossy magazines with half-finished crosswords and certain sentences of her mother's horoscope (Scorpio) underlined. In her parents' bedroom, there are photographs in silver frames – one of Dolores on the day of her first communion – rosary beads and a small porcelain dish with coins sitting on her mother's dressing table. Perfume bottles: round, rectangular, one with a long blue tassel. Her mother, every morning, in that fire-engine red dressing gown and the matching slippers. Lumpy white cream all over her face. A special cream she buys in bulk from a lady who turns up at the apartment once a month wheeling a fake crocodile-skin suitcase with cosmetics inside.

Who is this woman? Dolores began to wonder at age thirteen, about her mother, who was sitting opposite her at the dinner table, talking with her mouth full, saying: *I wish you wouldn't eat so much.* Often, and especially if Dolores' father was listening, she would add: *Everyone in my family is perfectly skinny, but, of course, who knows what genes come from your father's side.* Dolores' mother was particularly proud of her Spanish roots. She bought books by Spanish authors and put them on display in their apartment. They went unread. She had a strict diet that she departed from daily. She kept pink scales in the bathroom. Every morning, she talked to her sisters on the phone, cradling it in the nook of her neck while she made school lunches, saying: *It's not baby fat.* Saying: *From her father.* Saying: *It's already a problem.*

And Dolores' father? He was someone who went to bed after dinner and got up before sunrise for work. The kind of father who hid sweets from his wife to share with his children. A giver of both slaps and kisses. An angry man. An affectionate man. An orphan. It was something that he would not talk about, his youth. A secret subject. One that Dolores' mother would speak about in an exaggerated hushed whisper so that her voice wasn't really hushed at all. From her mother, Dolores knew that her father had been raised in a mission. Raised by Jesuit priests. *I can't tell you any more, you're too young,* is what Dolores' mother would say. Her father did not go to church but he prayed constantly. Little whisper prayers he said while driving or standing in the supermarket or at night before he went to bed. Dolores sometimes watched him through the crack of the bedroom door. That large man, on his knees, his brow furrowed and his hands clasped together, whispering. It was a powerful image. A man who could sometimes scare his children, now kneeling on the ground, surrendering to something higher. Her younger brother took his father's first name but it was Dolores who looked like him. Same eyes, same hair, same largeness.

In the apartment Dolores grew up in, everyone was attractive and rich or ugly and poor. The lighting was always the same – a soft, artificial glow. Her mother was obsessed with the telenovelas that played from three to five in the afternoons. In these half-hour shows, lovers turned out to be siblings, characters went in and out of comas, or disappeared completely, only to return several years later. There were runaway brides, evil twins and, yes, affairs that resulted in scandalous pregnancies. Most afternoons, Dolores' mother would watch the telenovelas with her neighbour – a widowed woman with a long, thin neck and her hair always in that dramatic bouffant on top of her head. The neighbour was a gossip. Every apartment block has one. This woman wore satin slippers. She made no noise when she walked. Hers was the only door with a peephole. During the telenovelas, but only in the commercial breaks, the two women would talk about the other people who lived in the building. The neighbour complained of what she called *night noises* coming from the apartment next to hers, in which a newly married couple lived. Although she had never seen it, she believed that the man who lived below her kept a dog. She swore she heard it barking. She was particularly suspicious of the divorced mother who lived in the apartment above. Watching the telenovelas and talking about their neighbours – to Dolores, these acts were inseparable. They fed off one another.

Those afternoons gave the two women the opportunity to assert their own sense of morality. Certain characters were good and certain characters were bad. This much was evident to Dolores, who noticed that whenever a bad character appeared on screen they emerged from the shadows with some kind of sinister music playing. An organ, perhaps, or some strings. Dolores' mother would hiss. For her, watching the telenovelas was the same as watching sport: there were winners and losers and sometimes she even swore, softly, under her breath.

After the telenovelas, in the late afternoons, Dolores would walk to Liliana's, stopping to buy a tub of ice-cream on the way. They lived in the same cluster of identical apartment blocks that sat just off the highway, next to a petrol station. Dolores would buy the ice-cream from the petrol station and then eat it sitting on the bench near the pump because she liked the smell. It was something about the combination. The sweetness of the ice-cream – cold, then melting in her mouth – and the petrol fumes thick in her nose. She would sit on the bench and watch cars come and go, exchanging ceremonious nods with children who looked longingly at her ice-cream while Dolores feigned nonchalance.

It really was the highlight of her life. The walk, the petrol station, the ice-cream. Her newly obtained independence.

She would climb the stairs, full and happy, and ring the bell. Liliana's mother would open the door and kiss her face. Big wet kisses. The smell of musk mixed with cigarettes and that warm husky laugh. In that apartment, it was just Liliana, her mother and the large portrait of Liliana's father that hung on the wall with a small shrine on the table below. Lace cloth, lit candles, dead petals, and, in the centre of it all, a fat gold wedding ring. No men's clothes. No masculine smells. No telenovelas playing on the television in that home. Liliana would be in her room, lovesick. For the past two years she had been in love with Jesus. Nightly, she had kissed the prayer card that sat in a frame by her bed. Now, at age eleven, Liliana was in love with the boy who worked at the petrol station. He was older. He had a small tuft of hair on his chin and his ears were pierced. Had they ever properly spoken? Dolores never asked. She knew that Liliana kept the receipts he handed her in a small wooden box with a lock. And she was happy to listen to Liliana ramble while her mother brought them treats (rice pudding and doughy rolls dusted with sugar) but her mind wandered while Liliana yapped.

On her walk home, Dolores sometimes saw a girl who used to go to her school pushing a stroller around the park. She knew her name. Only a year or so ago, they had sat together in class. Then, the girl left. And no one knew why. She went away and when she returned she was pushing a stroller around the park and Dolores pretended she didn't know who she was. It seemed like the polite thing to do. To address the girl would have been embarrassing. Still, she couldn't help but stare. This tiny girl. Thirteen years old and half the size of Dolores. With long legs and thin arms. Pushing a stroller with a big and – it's true – *ugly* baby strapped inside. He had an enormous head and thin lips. Old-man wrinkles. Who knew that a baby could snarl? When that baby cried, he sounded like he had bubbles in his throat. Like the monotonous gurgle of a crow.

AUGUST

In August, Dolores adjusts to the rhythm of the days at the convent. She knows, only from the calendar that hangs on the wall in the corner of the kitchen, that eight weeks have passed since she was carried in through the iron gates.

When the bells ring at five-thirty in the morning, everyone wakes, dresses, and makes their way to the chapel for morning prayer. At six-thirty, they eat breakfast: bread, tomatoes, and if it's available from the garden, fruit. Afterwards, they make their beds and clean the bathrooms. At eight, they meet again for prayer. At nine, Dolores meets the mother superior in the study room for lessons. At eleven, she joins the others in their chores. They tend the vegetable garden. They dust the chapel. They mop the dining-room floor. Sometimes, they knit or weave baskets. There are clothes to be washed and mended. Once a month, on a Thursday, the mother unlocks the gates and six of the strongest nuns go down to the bottom of the driveway with a wheelbarrow. They collect donations from the letter box: canned food, toilet paper, batteries, soap, sewing materials. At one, they eat lunch (soup or stew, bread). At two-thirty, they pray together in the chapel. From three to five, they may do what they please, but they must not leave the sitting room. At six, it's holy Mass. At seven-thirty, they eat dinner (variations of potato and corn dishes, and, on special occasions, canned fish). At nine, they pray together once more before bed. At nine-thirty, the lights go out.

There is the problem of food – of how little the nuns are expected to eat. How quietly they finish their meals. In the dining room, Dolores watches the way that the nuns bring their spoons to their mouths in slow motion. How they seem to *chew* the soup as if it were a piece of meat. The mother has told Dolores to try holding the soup in her mouth for twenty seconds before swallowing. All throughout the day, her stomach quivers. Her head feels light. She is constantly thirsty and she craves something sweet.

The nuns only shower on Saturdays. By the end

of summer, the room where Dolores sleeps smells of sweat. Nausea comes to Dolores in the mornings and in the kitchen when it's her turn to cook. She has woken up moments before the morning bells ring to be sick in the toilet on three occasions. She runs the taps to muffle the sound.

The days of the week blur. Time, at the convent, is measured by the bells that ring throughout the day, telling the nuns to move on to the next task. At the convent, the mother encourages the nuns to be alone with God. But physically they are never alone. Every chore is assigned in groups of two or more. The two hours of allocated free time in the afternoon is for sitting together. For sewing, for reading certain books, and for contemplation.

The nuns aren't allowed to go for walks. This was something Dolores learnt quickly. One afternoon, not long after she first arrived, she left the sitting room and went wandering up the hill behind the convent. She thought she might climb to the top and look out over the valley. The hill was steep – all wild shrubbery and rocks. Sticks poked at her ankles. Soon, she was on her hands and knees, clawing her way to the top. Little paper-like cuts on her hands. It felt good. Her skin stained with dirt and spots of dried blood on the palms of her hands. The thrill of possibly falling. She was halfway up when she heard the bells. When they didn't stop, she turned and sat on the hill, facing the convent below. In the distance, she saw a group of nuns running towards her with their arms flailing above their heads. She waved back but the nuns kept running. Soon, the bells abruptly stopped and it was completely silent. As the nuns got closer, Dolores noticed that they made no noise. They waved their arms but they did not yell. They didn't make a peep at all but their faces, even from across the landscape, seemed to scream: *Emergency!*

From certain windows, and from the wide balcony that runs along one side of the convent, Dolores can see a mountain in the distance. She knows the ocean is on the other side. On particularly clear days, Dolores has seen people jump from that mountain. Hang-gliders. They appear like large fluorescent birds on the horizon. They leap, and in those first few moments in the air, Dolores waits for them to drop. She imagines them plummeting to the ground. But they never do. They freeze in the air, suspended, then slowly make their way down.

One afternoon, at the end of August, Dolores is

outside gardening when she notices a man standing on the other side of the iron gates and feels her stomach drop. Her hands are covered in compost. She wipes her smock, stands, and squints. The man in the distance wears dark robes. One by one, the other nuns in the garden turn to face him. Then, the rhythmic jangling of the mother superior's keys, bouncing on the chain around her neck as she walks towards the gates. The moon-faced sister is the only one still crouching in the garden bed, her arms elbow-deep in soil. She whispers: *The bishop.* The mother unlocks the gates. Dolores kneels. Begins to turn the soil with her hands. The jangling of the keys once more and then the sound of crunching footsteps. In the corner of her eye, Dolores can see the mother superior's shoes – which must have been black once but are now greyish blue – and the bishop's shiny patent leather ones, walking towards her. They stop. She keeps her eyes on the mother's shoes. They look so small. They are bound together by black tape at the toe. *Do-lor-es*, the mother says and Dolores tilts her face towards the sun. There he is, the bishop. Looking down at Dolores in the garden bed. He has a face like wet lettuce. He wears round, tinted glasses that obscure his eyes. *Child,* the bishop says, and then something about Dolores *arriving all the way from the tropics*. Dolores nods. All Dolores ever does is nod. She notices that his hands, which are clasped together and resting on his belly, are shaking.

That night, hours after the lights have gone out, Dolores wakes up covered in sweat. Heat is radiating off her body. In the bathroom, she runs the taps and quickly vomits. She pours cold water down her back. When she returns to the room, she notices that the moon-faced sister isn't in her bed. She tries to sleep but there is movement all around her. Rustling covers, and every so often the groan of mattress springs. When she does fall asleep, Dolores hears the morning bells ring. And as before, the sound enters into her dream.

It's a small room with dark-green carpet, like moss. Two towels, twisted into the shape of two swans kissing, are displayed on the bed. An alarm rings through the speakers on the wall, announcing when the hour is over. At fifteen, Dolores began to visit the love motels on the outskirts of her city. Now, at night inside the convent, when she returns, the different rooms have merged into one.

The bed is circular. Six panels of mirror surround the mattress in a half-hexagon. The sheets are off-white and yellowing. It looks like an open clam. A fan points down from the ceiling. There are tissues and stale chocolates on a small brass table. Fake ferns in the bathroom, golden fixtures and dark wood panelling. Everything inside the room is dusty red from the neon hearts that line the wall. From the highway, you can see the red lights in the windows. You can see the billboards – painted silhouettes of lips or a woman's parted legs – advertising rooms by the hour.

The love motels, when did she find out what they were? In a way, Dolores always knew. She knew from the red lights in the windows. From the hush that entered the car whenever her family passed one on the highway. She knew, but she still needed confirmation. So, she asked. *A love motel?* her older cousin once said, pausing to choose her words carefully, *It is a place you go to make love.* Liliana's mother told them it was a motel for businesswomen from out of town. And Dolores' mother? *They're for prostitutes and adulterers.* And later: *They're run by whores.* That was all it took. From the bench by the petrol station, Dolores could see the red lights of one of the motels in the distance. And she wanted nothing more than to see what was inside.

The first time Dolores visited a love motel it was with the boy from her cousin's fifteenth birthday party. The one with the green jumper. They hadn't spoken that night. But in the years between she had seen him from afar – at the supermarket, at the petrol station, in the park by her school. And perhaps the other boys had talked to him about her. The ones from behind the red curtain. Maybe they had mentioned how obliging Dolores had been. In the beginning, she didn't mind being talked about, especially to the boy with the green jumper.

His name is Angelo. He wears a thin gold chain with a small crucifix around his neck. When they meet again, Angelo is eighteen. He has a girlfriend. The same girl who sat on the table in the church basement. Do they visit the same love motels? Is she as obliging? This is what Dolores wonders and decides that the answer must be no. Otherwise, why would he be driving by her school in the afternoons and offering to give her a ride home in his nice car? A silver car, with speakers in the back. Inside, it smells of cologne and leather.

There were times they used the car as a room too. Angelo would drive up to the old stretch of highway, now barely used, that led to the top of a mountain overlooking their city. At the top, there was an outdoor car park obscured from the road by some trees, a bench, some bins, and a small, unused chapel. Dolores thought it was beautiful. From the car park they could see the city below them – rows of buildings and sprawling highways stretching out from the centre. At sunset, the sky would turn a ridiculous pink and then everything went dark except for the city lights below. It might have been romantic, up there, on the mountain, but Angelo was overprotective of his car. Neurotic about stains and smells. In fact, he had a preoccupation with cleanliness overall.

In the moss-green room, he would bolt to the shower immediately after they finished. And those few minutes, while Dolores sat alone on the bed, a patch of wetness forming underneath her, listening to the shower run, were the only time she had any sense of discomfort. An unwelcome feeling. Some might call it shame. She would run her tongue over her crooked teeth, as if to confirm their position. Angelo would emerge from the shower with a towel over his shoulder. The feeling would pass. Clean and confident, he would stride back to the bed. Then, and only then, was he ever tender. Affectionate. After they finished, and after he showered.

Women have cycles, that's what Angelo told her, they go by the moon. At certain times of each month it was perfectly safe. There was no chance of conception. He told her that cars once ran on whale oil. That it was illegal to drive a dirty car in Russia. He told her all about the legendary bull Diablo – how it was the name of his favourite car. He seemed to know all kinds of things. So, they went by the moon. Which is to say that the moon dictated what they did in the love motels. They developed a routine. It was, for Dolores, a new afternoon ritual. Six months passed quickly, with Angelo driving up and down different stretches of highway, taking her to the mountain or to a motel.

It was during this time, in the moss-green room, after they had fallen asleep in the afternoon light and woken up in the dark, that Angelo told Dolores about his father and the new family he was raising in another city, three hours away. His father had two young sons. They were twins. Two brothers that Angelo would never meet. He had seen them once, from the inside of his mother's car, when the boys were just babies. Dolores listened to his voice and then looked for his hand in the dark. She felt her heart swell. It wasn't for Angelo but for herself – for the secret he had gifted her. She turned it over carefully in her head, swore that she would guard it with her life, and then said a little prayer of thanks.

Because Dolores knew all about secrets. She thought of them as something she had to protect. About the motel visits, she only told Liliana, and she sugar-coated what went on. In this way, the motel visits became the most monumental secret of all. There was a lot of planning involved. She told all kinds of lies. She took great risks for those few hours. And her heart never went so fast as it did when she approached the front door of her apartment, and she imagined her mother inside, standing by the door, waiting for her to come home, knowing what she had done. Her face burned red whenever she passed one of the motels with her parents. The secret fed something. It gave her a new identity. It was something to think about late at night in bed or in the morning when she first woke up. It was always with her. Comforting, is what it was.

Then it was summer, the last day of the school year, and Dolores was waiting for Angelo on the dead-end street that was their secret pick-up spot. The silver car approached with another boy inside. He was sitting in the passenger's seat where Dolores normally sat, with the windows rolled down. The car stopped beside her. *Hello,* said the boy. Angelo was in the driver's seat, talking on his new toy, a mobile phone. He flicked his head towards the back and Dolores quickly got in. They drove out towards the highway and Dolores smoothed her skirt. Her hands were shaking from excitement. Because here was something new: an introduction! Here was Angelo letting her into his world. Now, there were three of them. Dolores, Angelo, and the friend. And perhaps they would go to that café she had heard so much about.

The sun was strong and shining. It was a beautiful day. A new kind of confidence overtook her. *Somebody give me a cigarette,* she said. The boy in the front obliged. Angelo, who was still talking on his phone, and who didn't like her to smoke, was frowning. *Turn the music up!* Dolores said, now ecstatic, but then quickly added: *Please.* The boy up front followed through with her request. Angelo hung up the phone. Dolores was smoking in the back with the window rolled down and her hair was blowing in the wind. (Who am I? she was thinking.) *Well,* she said, leaning in between the two front seats to address both boys, *Are we going to have a little drink?* Angelo caught her reflection in the mirror. *Maybe, maybe,* he said. *But first I have to pick something up. I'll be an hour or something, you two can keep each other company until I get back.* An electric pause. Dolores knew immediately what he meant.

The car pulled into their regular motel. The boy got out. Dolores was still sitting in the back. Angelo turned to her and did something small but mighty: he winked. It was a wink that said: *Everything is OK.* Or it was a wink that said: *This is just a joke.* Or it was a wink that said: *I love you.* Dolores got out. Angelo revved his car. She watched him pull out onto the road. Briefly, she felt something claw at her heart. The feeling passed. She watched the car disappear into the distance and then turned to the boy standing beside her. He had thin arms and long legs. Sporadic black hairs on his chin and cheeks. Thick eyebrows. He was looking down at his feet. Dolores took his hand. *We better go inside,* she said.

Inside the motel, the hour passed quickly. And Dolores was happy, doing what she knew how to do. When Angelo returned, the three of them really did have a drink. They sat in the back room of the café she had heard so much about and music was playing and Dolores was drinking a beer and she was happy, even though she was pretending to like the taste.

After that first time, over the summer, sometimes Angelo came alone and sometimes he had a friend in the front seat. To Dolores, they were different-looking boys who, after a while, all seemed the same. At first, they were cocky, boastful, and at times unpleasant during the drive. But alone, in the motel room with Dolores, something would shift. Their body language would change. Their way of speaking too. There would be a bright, unmistakable moment of vulnerability. Some kind of stumbling. An apology. This happened without fail. And it made Dolores feel powerful, as if she had the upper hand. It was mesmerising, this effect she could have on another person. She looked at what went on in the motel rooms from above, somehow outside of herself, in disbelief.

She began to appreciate their different bodies. Thin waists and long backs. The thick and curly hair on their bellies. Big shoulders and thighs. All of these things suddenly within reach.

You're a sweet girl, they told her. *So generous, such a big heart!* They liked to squeeze handfuls of flesh. Sometimes they said: *I love your big body.*

After the motel visits, they would drop her at the petrol station or somewhere nearby. And Dolores, high on all the compliments, would practically float up the stairs on her walk to Liliana's. There, she would sit on the bed, and Liliana, who was often Dolores' alibi, would listen with her head down. Liliana was scared of sex. Lying made her nervous. She did not want to be complicit in the sin. Dolores listed some of the things that they did. She said it casually. She liked the look on her cousin's face. But she withheld everything when it came to Angelo. There was pleasure in this. In withholding a secret that belonged to her and Angelo alone.

SEPTEMBER

SEPTEMBER

Inside the convent, on the wall in the dining room, there is a large sign that reads: '*Silentium*'. The rule is strictly enforced. If necessary, the nuns speak using coded gestures of the hand. They motion for soup or for extra bread. Any unnecessary noise is considered vulgar. The sound of a spoon hitting the side of a bowl. Heavy footsteps in the corridors. The legs of a chair dragged across the floor. Once, when Dolores accidently slammed the large wooden door on her way into the dining room, some of the nuns dropped to their knees. Pure horror flashed across their faces. It was as if a bomb had fallen from the sky. One nun stood frozen in the middle of the room with her hands covering her ears.

But outside of the dining room, away from the mother superior, things are different.

When Dolores arrived at the convent, she already knew, from those afternoons with her mother and neighbour, that even the most pious women cannot resist the temptation of gossip. By September, she discovers that the less she speaks, the more others will divulge. She discovers that all she has to do is be in the same room. So, in the kitchen, while she washes the dishes from lunch in a sink full of lumpy water, she is listening. In the garden, while the nuns weed the garden and rake the leaves, she is listening. When Dolores is alone with one other nun, in the sewing room or when dusting the chapel, she listens while the other talks. She hardly participates. It's the older ones that want to chat. Given the opportunity, their mouths open easily. Most of the nuns, Dolores has noticed, mutter quietly to themselves as they walk through the corridors of the convent.

They're sentimental, the older nuns. But any sentiment for life before the walls of the convent is a sin. So they tell Dolores about the day they took their final vows. There is one nun who paints herself as a giddy bride. She has told this story so often that Dolores knows it off by heart. She sits beside the nun in the damp laundry, surrounded by soapy buckets, while they wash smocks, socks and underwear. The nun is old and sweet and gangly-looking. She has large teeth and her jaw juts out beyond her chin. Because of the jaw, and the saliva she produces when she talks, the nun often has to stop and swallow. Dolores feels a kind of kinship with the nun and her awkward jaw. She is never not aware of her own bad teeth. When Dolores laughs, she instinctively covers her mouth. The gangly nun gulps down her spit unashamedly. This is how her story goes: On the day that she took her final vows, she woke up early, around four, filled with excitement. It was early spring, and she was smiling so much her cheeks hurt. The other nuns entered the room and covered her in lace. She wore a crown of thorns on her head. She was twenty-seven years old. During the ceremony, when she lay on the ground to kiss the floor, her heart felt full and her body felt weightless. She says she has carried that lightness around with her ever since. Dolores keeps her eyes lowered while the nun talks. Her hands are in the bucket swirling the dirty water around. Her own body feels big and bloated underneath her brown smock. Her stomach bubbles. She lets out a silent fart. The smell mixes with the soap. The nun stops to swallow. Her eyes are bright. She truly is the most joyful person Dolores has ever met.

One day, in the laundry again, the joyful nun

confides in Dolores that she once fell in love. It was decades ago, she says, when she was thirty-four years old. A young man had come to stay at the convent while he fixed the plumbing. He was twenty-three years old. It went against all of her beliefs, loving this man. But she thought about him constantly. She went out of her way to walk past him while he worked. In her mind, they had long conversations about their lives and revealed their most secret wishes. It went on like this for weeks. He slept in a room on the bottom floor of the convent. A kind of cleaning closet that the mother superior had put a mattress in. And each night when she went to bed, the joyful nun could not sleep because she knew he was just below her. Then, one day, when she walked past him, he asked her to show him where the water had been leaking in the basement. That was all it took. After that, they spoke every single day. She stood beside him with her head bowed down while he worked. When the mother superior summoned the joyful nun to her office, she lied and told the mother that she was talking to the young man about God. It was her first lie. She convinced the mother that the man needed guidance. In fact, he was asking her questions about her life. How young was she when she entered, he wanted to know, did she know about the kinds of things she had missed? One day, he kissed her. A short kiss. Barely a brush on the lips. She walked away and kept her hand on her mouth, which was tingling for the next hour. After the kiss, everything changed. The kiss offered her an image of another life. Then, not long after, he was gone. He left without saying goodbye.

For seven years, the joyful nun thought about this man. She questioned her vows. For the first time in her life, she was angry. Then, one day during prayer, she felt the same lightness in her body again. And she realised that it had been missing all those years. The young man had been a test. This is what she now knows. As soon as she realised, she felt released. She kissed the ground with the same intensity that she had on the day she took her vows.

When the joyful nun's confession was over, Dolores did what she always did when someone offered her a secret. She gently turned it over in her head. Said a quick prayer of thanks. But a thought wandered over from the other side of her mind: Who would plant a kiss on that slack jaw? She quickly pushed the thought aside.

The oldest nun at the convent is ninety-three

years old. She hardly does anything at all. She prays and she eats. She sleeps in her special chair in the sitting room. She is not a joyful nun. *The world is in so much trouble,* she often tells Dolores, *because it's godless. Without God,* she says, *people have filled themselves up on the garbage of the world. People today are garbage-eaters,* she says. The ninety-three-year-old nun smells like cabbage. Her eyes are bloodshot and she chews her lips. *God loves you,* she tells Dolores, waggling her finger, *but he wants your love in return.*

In September, Dolores overhears some of the nuns talking about the bishop. He is a nun-lover, they say, and smile. Here is something else that she learns. At another convent, across the border, a forty-two-year-old nun gave birth to a baby boy. They say she just turned up at that convent one day. No one knows exactly how she got there. And no one will use the word for what happened to her. Besides, some of the nuns don't believe it. They don't believe that a priest would do such a thing. *This woman,* they say, and they say the word *woman* as if it were a question. As if such a woman didn't exist. *Maybe,* one of the older nuns says, in a whisper, *maybe the priest was coerced by some kind of black magic.* Her mouth goes taut. Her eyes light up. *They have that kind of thing where you're from, don't they, Dolores?*

At the end of September, Dolores quietly turns seventeen. She has been at the convent for three months. At five-thirty in the morning, when the nuns wake up, the sky outside is blue-black. In the dim light of a lamp across the room, the nuns dress. Dolores lingers in bed, pretending not to watch. Their skin is soft and dimpled. She wonders how long it has been since certain parts of their bodies saw the sun. When the nuns rush out of the room – tut tut tutting at Dolores on their way out for taking so long – Dolores finally gets out of bed. She layers herself in clothes. She rarely showers any more. In the bathroom sink, she washes her face and wonders what she looks like. There are no mirrors in the bathroom. No mirrors anywhere inside the convent at all. Dolores only sees her face when she walks past a window at night. It always surprises her. That blurry flash of a face that is supposed to be her.

On the day of her birthday, Dolores is cleaning the study room with the moon-faced sister when she stops to look out the window at her mountain and sees, below her, the mother superior walking to the iron gates. The mother unlocks the gates and they groan loudly as she pulls them open. Walking up the driveway, towards the mother, is a girl in a long red coat. She's dragging a small suitcase. She has a large bag strapped across her back.

There was a lack of blood. Which is a strange indication of life to come. It was easy to ignore, at first. Dolores thought about it briefly and then continued with her routine. Only by then it had changed a little.

When school first returned after the summer, she would wait at the secret pick-up spot on the dead-end street near her school and Angelo would arrive swiftly in his silver car. Sometimes on his own, sometimes with a friend in the front seat. They would drive to the love motels. This new routine went on for a month, maybe more. Then, one day, Angelo didn't show, and Dolores waited for three hours. Late at night, at the hour he allowed her to call his mobile, Dolores stood in the kitchen, twisting the cord of the home phone around her fingers until the tips turned white. The call rang out. Her family were asleep. She dialled fourteen times more.

She tried not to think of the phone bill that her father would eventually open. Those midnight calls. Angelo never picked up.

The next time she saw him, he was annoyed. He was at work, he said (he worked at a butcher's shop that seemed to keep strange hours). Then he told her never to call again. He complained of his boss calling him all the time. Of his mother constantly asking where he was. It became normal that Dolores never knew if he was going to turn up at all. Still, she went to the spot on their regular days of the week and waited, sometimes for over an hour, trying not to look up too eagerly each time she heard the sound of a car approaching. Because sometimes he did show up, with apologies and rambling stories, and all that mattered by then was that he'd arrived at all. The waiting, it truly was the worst part. Not knowing when to give in. Kicking rocks and smoking cigarettes. This was how Dolores passed the time. Plucking all the flowers from the nice gardens that lined the street. Scrunching them up in her fist. On the occasions when he did not come, the sun would go down and Dolores would give up waiting. Then, having missed the last bus, she would walk home along the highway.

It took about two hours, the walk. She had to pass the bridge where the sleepy-eyed people her mother had another name for slept. Her mother would have killed her if she had seen Dolores walking along the highway. The worst part was when she had to pass the half-built hospital, now abandoned. It was a cement structure with curved archways and vines crawling up the walls. A wheelbarrow and some bricks stacked out the front. Rubbish strewn everywhere. From the outside, it looked like the inside of a body. The wooden frames were the bones. Red and blue tarps (the organs, water, blood and guts) fluttered in the wind. Sometimes, walking past the hospital, Dolores felt cold hands at the back of her neck. Her heart would race. But nothing was there. Once, when she was walking by, she heard voices calling out from inside. *Hello,* they said. *Hey! Hello!* That's all they said.

It was on one of these walks, as a storm rolled in, when a car slowed down on the highway and a familiar voice called out her name. It was the boy from the petrol station. Liliana's unrequited love. With the little tuft of hair on his chin. Here he was, his car driving slowly beside her with the window rolled down, offering her a ride home. Thunder cracked. The rain fell in heavy drops. Dolores looked at the lightning in the distance, shrugged and got into the passenger's seat. He was on his way to work. He asked her what she was doing walking along the highway. *I just like to walk,* she told him. *It's dangerous,* he said solemnly. And as they drove through the rain in silence, she looked at him and thought to herself: what would a sweet girl like Liliana do with an idiot like that? Nothing, she guessed. He wanted to drive her to her front door. Dolores insisted that it was safer for them both if he stopped around the corner. He made her promise not to walk alone on the highway again. She put a hand to her heart and swore that she wouldn't. But a week or so later, when Angelo forgot to pick her up, she found herself walking along the same stretch of highway, waiting to hear her name being called, as indeed it was.

Amidst all of this – the lack of blood and what to do about it. A month had passed. Late at night, Dolores found herself indulging in fantasises that would embarrass her in waking hours. A white gown, the thought of no longer having to live with her mother, a small seat in the back of Angelo's silver car. Ridiculous, she thought. But then, at night, as these images played on a loop in her head, a new voice emerged. *Maybe,* it said, *maybe.*

It happened one day after school, at the end of May. Dolores had been waiting on the dead-end street for half an hour. She heard his car and felt the corners of her mouth twitch with pleasure. She got in the front seat and Angelo drove them to the top of the mountain. As they circled their way up, Dolores looked out at the edge of the road, thick with trees. They parked in their usual spot by the chapel. No one else was around. They were above the city, looking down at the buildings, and the zigzagged highways sprawling out in each direction. It was there, in the car, that late afternoon as the sun began to set, that Dolores first gave what might be happening in her body a name. It was the first time she uttered the word out loud. Her voice went to a high, unfamiliar place. *I was thinking,* she said, and then she said: *baby.* She said: *What if we had a baby?* She said it in the way that someone might say: *What if we shared a pizza?* His reaction was swift, definitive: *I wouldn't want that.* A terrible silence followed. *Are you crazy?* he said, and then: *What is this?* Sitting side by side in the car, Dolores could sense the space between them widening. It was nothing, she said, just a little joke. She had wanted to scare him. *It wouldn't scare me,* he said quickly. He rattled off names, counting on his fingers as he said them. He was listing the boys who had sat in the front seat of his car. *How would you even know it was mine?* he said. Dolores told him: *I don't let them do what you do.* His face changed. Then, that horrible silence again. Outside the car, the sun had almost set and the lights in the city were beginning to appear: dim twinkles on the horizon. Angelo was looking straight ahead. *If you tell anyone about us,* he said, *I'll deny it.* He tapped his fingers on the steering wheel. *What is this?* he said again. Dolores looked at his hands on the wheel. The silver rings he wore on three of his fingers. The rosary beads that hung from the rear-view mirror, tangled up with a tree-shaped air freshener. The car smelt like pine, cigarettes, and Angelo's cologne. She knew the smell so well. He sniffed, *Get out.* Dolores sat still. *I'm serious,* he said. Dolores got out and Angelo drove away.

She waited for him to return. She was certain he would. She waited until it was completely dark. Then, because she did not know what else to do, she began to walk down the mountain. She followed the curve of the road. She kept to the very edge, feeling for the thick trees beside her. There were no street lamps. Every so often, lights flashed behind her and she heard an angry beep, the swerve of tyres. Drivers, every single one of them resembling Angelo, yelled out the window as they passed: *Are you crazy?* One car finally stopped. Inside was a man old enough to be her grandfather. He got out of the car and opened the door for her. She told him where she lived and he drove her home without asking questions. A small kindness.

When Dolores walked into the apartment, her family were already eating. She sat down at the table with her mother, father, and brother and their words floated somewhere above her. One thousand images passed through her head. Among them: herself, in the future, walking around the park like the girl from school. She saw herself walking down mountain after mountain alone. Out of nowhere, a word spoken at the dinner table smacked her in the face. It came from her mother's mouth. Dolores looked up.

Pregnant, her mother said. Her mother was talking about her niece, Dolores' cousin, now married and living in Spain. The cousin was depressed because she wasn't pregnant. *She needs female company,* her mother said.

Later that night, after everyone had gone to bed, Dolores sat on the floor of the kitchen and dialled

Angelo's number. The call rang out. She dialled again. How many times did she call before his phone was switched off? Twenty, maybe more.

OCTOBER

The new girl arrives. She has a perfect oval face, small pink lips, and long fingernails. Straight teeth. Blonde hair that curls in tight ringlets. She looks like a thin, teenage cherub. The new girl arrives, and everything at the convent buzzes. Everyone is now looking at themselves through the eyes of the new girl. It's as if the nuns have been living in one long nap and now they are suddenly awake. They carry out their tasks – cooking, cleaning, walking, even praying – with extra vivacity. Now, the nuns kiss the mother superior's hand every morning. They acknowledge one another in the corridors with a nod that is both solemn and divine. They cover the ninety-three-year-old nun in blankets and turn her chair to face the wall.

The new girl arrives and Dolores cannot help but see the convent anew. She notices the things she first noticed about the convent many months ago. The dignified beauty of the chapel at first light in the morning, the way the stained-glass windows tint the room. The grandeur of the arched balcony in the middle of the day when the sun hits the sandstone and everything turns gold. The quietness of the place. Nothing but mountain after mountain in the distance. *What a view!* the new girl says as she tours the grounds, arm in arm with the mother superior. *What a place to live,* she says, *above the clouds, so close to heaven!*

In the chapel, when the new girl prays, she whispers fiercely and tears fall down her face. On her first full day at the convent, she refuses extra bread at lunch and a wave of silent approval floods the room. After lunch, she offers to do extra chores. There she is: the new girl, in the damp and badly lit bathroom, on her hands and knees, scouring the tiles with a bleach-soaked brush. There she is in the garden, dragging an axe behind her as she goes to chop the wood. What noise she makes! Little dramatic yelps emerge from her tiny body as she brings the axe down. Who would have guessed she had such strength? Because she is a dainty thing, the new girl.

She has brought a small guitar to the convent and the mother allows her to play. Those long fingernails

– they're for plucking the strings. In the sitting room, in the late afternoons, she lets the other nuns hold the guitar. She shows them where to place their fingers on the fretboard. She hums and ooohs and ahhhs.

The new girl joins Dolores and the mother superior for lessons. She appears to have memorised the Bible front to back. Each time the new girl answers a question, Dolores studies the mother superior's face. Her mouth is half open, in ecstasy. The mother looks drunk with pride. They are chick and hen, the new girl and the mother superior. At the convent, they need younger girls. They need new nuns to continue their work. And Dolores knows, she can tell from the mother's eyes, that the new girl is a serious candidate. Selfless, with seemingly no hunger at all. At lunch, she continues to refuse bread. She takes only the smallest portion of soup. She only ever eats half of an apple and then nurses the other half for the remainder of the day, pausing to take tiny bites. Whenever Dolores eyes the new girl's browning apple, a feeling of intense rage rises from her gut.

On her fifth day at the convent, during study hours, the new girl insists on massaging the mother's feet. Dolores watches silently as the new girl kneels on the floor by the mother and delicately removes her old, greying shoes, her holey socks. The mother is giggling like an idiot. Dolores has only ever seen the mother's face and hands. Now, without her socks on, and the skin of her feet exposed, the mother appears almost naked. Her feet are translucent white against the brown carpet and they look as though they've been soaking in a bath for several years. Shrivelled. With thick blue veins. Her two smallest toes cross over one another. Her toenails are black and green. Gracefully, the new girl lifts the mother's foot and rests it on top of her knee. She uses her thumbs and fingers and those long fingernails to knead the mother's doughy flesh. After a while, Dolores leaves the room.

What do they know about her, the new girl? She is the only child of semi-famous parents. Her mother is a solo soprano in the touring Sacred Heart Choir. Her father is the only heir of a wealthy oil tycoon. This is what the nuns whisper. The family have made large donations to the church. Together, the three of them have moved, country to country, mission to mission. Mother and daughter performing hymns. Carrying bricks and building schools. There are images of the new girl in the glossy brochures and newsletters put out by different missions. Those big dimples, little splashes of mud on her arms, posing somewhere in the thick of the Amazon, holding up a cross.

At the convent, the new girl sings all day and the mother superior encourages it. The nuns hear her voice echoing throughout the corridors. She sings in the kitchen while she cooks. She sings in the laundry and in the chapel. She even sings in the bathroom, on the toilet, with the door closed. Her voice is clean, perfectly pitched, and soulless.

After a week, the new girl starts to receive mail. Three or four letters at a time. *Pen pals,* the new girl says. *I'm in dialogue with little angels around the world.* The letters come from Benin, Trinidad and Tobago, Bulgaria, Cameroon. Now, at night, after dinner, Dolores listens when the mother superior calls out the names of the nuns who have received letters. Why? Nobody knows exactly where she is. Yet, that doesn't stop her from thinking her name might be called.

One day, at the end of their study, and only after the new girl has left the room, Dolores tells the mother superior that she wants to write a letter.

The mother smiles. Her teeth are yellow. *Do-lor-es,* she says. Then she asks if Dolores is having second thoughts about taking her vows. Dolores shakes her head. The mother leaves the room. When she returns, she is holding a small envelope and a page of stamps. *Sit,* the mother says as she licks a stamp. *Address the envelope first,* she says. Dolores begins to write her home address. Halfway through, she pauses and crosses it out. *I've made a mistake,* she says. At this, the mother sucks her cheeks in like a fish. *We do not waste,* she says, softly. Dolores begins again. This time, she addresses the envelope to Liliana. She is waiting for a bit of privacy to write her letter, but the mother does not leave. They lock eyes. They lock eyes for a long time. *Dolores,* the mother says, *begin your letter.* A thought flickers across Dolores' mind. The mother is old and mad, Dolores thinks. Then she says a quick, silent prayer to apologise for the thought. She has her pen in her hand, paused at the top of the page. She knows that the mother is expecting a certain kind of letter. So, Dolores writes descriptions of her surroundings. She writes about the chapel. She writes the name of the convent in capital letters at the bottom. *God be with you,* she writes and signs her name – her real name. The mother sighs. *Any other letters to write, my child?* There is a look on the mother's face that she does not recognise. Dolores shakes her head. The mother pats her on the back, holds out her hand for the letter, folds it twice and places it in the envelope. She licks the envelope with her grey tongue and seals it shut.

In the middle of October, a dense fog appears. It obscures Dolores' view of the mountain. After two days, it covers everything. Inside the convent, from the study window, Dolores can only see as far as the iron gates. When the rain finally arrives, it is heavy and relentless. The convent leaks. The nuns place buckets and bowls throughout the building to catch the drips. There are soggy towels on the floor. Everything smells like a wet dog. During the night, Dolores wakes up four or five times to urinate. The air is muggy. Steam rises from the toilet. She presses her face against the cool tiles of the bathroom wall. During the nights when it rains, she dreams vividly. Her dreams are about letters. About volcanoes erupting inside her body.

It rains for two weeks straight. On the last day, it pours. The nuns are gathered in the sitting room. The roof is leaking and the drip comes in intervals of three seconds. It echoes around the room. Dolores is drawing on the foggy window with her finger. Stick figures and love hearts. The new girl is teaching the moon-faced girl how to play the guitar. They are sitting together on the floor at the other end of the room. *Yes, no,* she's saying, *not that way. Yes, and hold this finger down. Oh, my! You've got it. And pluck this string with this finger. Yes, exactly. Again? Do you hear that note? Ahhh –* she sings. *Yes, that's right. Bravo. Ahhh. And if you want to go higher – Ahhh, do you hear that? Ahhh –* the new girl is singing with her eyes closed and her angelic face pointed towards the heavens. From across the room, Hang Tooth gets up and strides towards them, nostrils flaring like a bull, and, without saying a word, grabs the guitar and brings it down on the new girl's head.

That crash – the sound of a guitar splitting in two – what strange music it made. No such sound has entered the convent since Dolores arrived. The new girl holds her face in her hands. Outside, the rain continues to fall. Everyone in the room is frozen. The new girl takes her hands away. Crimson, inky blood runs out of her nose. *Madonna!* the nuns whisper. The joyful, gangly nun with the unfortunate jaw swallows loudly. The new girl looks up, dazed. She brings her hand up to her nose and wipes the blood. Then, she begins to cry. Long, blubbering, rhythmic cries. Like an animal mating. The mother superior enters the room. Everyone turns. Hang Tooth stands still, resilient, with the broken guitar still in her hands.

She leaves two days later, the new girl. She has stayed barely a month. The mother superior walks her to the gates. They embrace. Dolores joins some of the other nuns as they watch from the balcony. There are lights in the distance. A large car arrives at the bottom of the driveway – an image of the new girl's wealth. Of everything the convent will lose. A man wearing all black gets out. He takes the new girl's suitcase. She gets inside and rolls the window down. Briefly, she glances up at the balcony.

Hang Tooth is punished. After the incident, she is no longer allowed in the sitting room in the hours between three and five. She is given extra chores. The mother superior has set her the task of gluing the guitar back together. The task is symbolic. The new girl did not wish to take the broken, tainted object. The guitar will never sound the same again. Yet, there she sits – Hang Tooth – in the study room, bent over the fractured pieces. She is just the same as always. Surly. One day, after morning prayer, the mother talks at length to the nuns about the act of forgiveness. She forgives Hang Tooth. The convent returns to how it was before the new girl arrived.

Not long after Angelo had left her alone at the top of the mountain, there was a dance. This is what Dolores pushes to the edge of her mind at night in the convent when sleep seems impossible: the dance and all the images that belong to it. Broken bottles, dead wet leaves, and those sticky magazines that the builders must have left before they abandoned the hospital. Fold-out chairs. Silver insulation glimmering on the walls.

The boys brought torches and portable speakers. Maybe the magazines belonged to them too. They hung sheets from the wooden frames to section off the different rooms. Outside, there were girls – the older ones who used to go to Dolores' school – walking up the muddy path, ruining their perfectly white sneakers. Girls trembling with bare shoulders; their jackets tied casually around the waist. Some girls with no jackets at all. It was

June, the beginning of winter, and the cold metal of their heavy jewellery must have felt like ice against the skin. That long line of girls standing outside in the cold, waiting to approach the half-built hospital. And the boys inside, waiting to receive them.

Liliana, eating the pink lipstick off her mouth and determined, so determined, that night to consummate her unrequited love affair with the boy from the petrol station. Liliana, now almost fifteen, had been vying for his attention for years. Only children are ruthless when it comes to competing for love. Competition is alien. They fear the unknown. Liliana was always imagining enemies. Imagining confrontations with non-existent girls she thought might steal his heart. Dolores went along with it out of private guilt. Those afternoons, in the car, with the boy from the petrol station, and the recent times they had visited the motels, were yet another secret Dolores had to keep. Perhaps the most important one of all.

Dolores did not want to go to the dance. She went for Liliana. She went because she thought her mother had been looking at her strangely. Lately, her mother had been having one of her monthly migraines and her father was in the middle of what Dolores' mother referred to as his *sleepy depressions*. Her father was, in this way, absent from the family. Still, Dolores overcompensated. She played with her brother. She swung him around the room like she used to when he was three. She read him stories until he told her, yawning, that he was no baby and the stories were embarrassing for them both. At night, while everyone slept, she went to the kitchen and held the phone up to her ear. The calls rang out.

On the night of the dance, Dolores and Liliana invented reasons for leaving, ran hot irons over their long hair, kissed their mothers on the cheek, and then met at the petrol station where they quickly changed their clothes. Walking along the highway, they passed a bottle of fizzy wine back and forth. It tasted like off fruit. Both sour and sweet. Dolores chugged on the bottle until it ran out the sides of her mouth. (Why not, why not, why not? she was thinking.) Car lights were flashing and horns were beeping and the trees shook with the wind. *Look,* Liliana said, wiggling her eyebrows up and down as she reached into her backpack and pulled out a second bottle of wine. After an hour of walking, they were drunk. From the wine and from the cold wind on their face and the creeping feeling that they might get caught. When they got to the empty stretch of highway where the abandoned hospital sat, they stashed their overnight bags under a tree and joined the other girls waiting to climb over the gate.

Inside the hospital there were shadows on the wall, warm heat radiating from dancing bodies, and a damp, fungus-like smell that permeated throughout the building. The bass from the speakers made the hospital shudder and a rumour went around that the building was not strong enough to hold them all. That it would soon collapse. Dolores, shivering inside, with her jacket now tied at her waist, said a secret prayer of thanks in anticipation that it would. For the past week or so, she had made similar prayers. To be hit by a car. To swallow a fish bone. To fall down the stairs. Anything. Then, she would say another prayer immediately after as an apology for thinking such a thing.

Liliana immediately went in search of the boy from the petrol station. Dolores stood in a corner and looked around the room. She picked up a bottle from the floor and began to drink. Something tasted rancid in her mouth and she immediately spat it out. Shadows danced on the walls. The earth shook. Or maybe it was her head that twirled. There they were. All of the boys Dolores had privately known in the different rooms of the love motels. Dancing. Holding and kissing hands. Performing dainty, gentlemanly actions. It made her laugh. She was laughing out loud. After a while, they were rubbing their bodies all over the girls they publicly labelled their lovers. And those girls, the official lovers, giggling! Like babies. The boys smiling, winking, bowing. Acting like mere servants to their masters. Dolores was standing in the corner alone, watching. Once or twice, they met her eye and then quickly looked away. And she had to remind herself that she knew their bodies. Had seen them so close. Knew about moles and birthmarks and scars. About muscles and hair and holes. Everything.

Dolores was waiting for Angelo. Waiting for him to enter the room with an aura of light vibrating around his head. Horns playing. An entrance someone might make in the telenovelas her mother watched. *Ridiculous, ridiculous*, she said out loud and to no one in particular but herself. She shook her head. She was indulging in images her drunkenness forgot to censor. White dress and the small seat in the back of the nice silver car. *You're drunk,* she told herself, out loud. She was thinking Angelo might enter the room and hold her hand. She was seeing him in the face of every boy who appeared in the doorway.

The night rolled on. She suddenly became aware that the dance floor had changed. No one was dancing. She was, in fact, lying on the ground, looking at the ceiling. All of a sudden, Dolores felt something surge in her stomach and climb up her throat. She got on her hands and knees and crawled aimlessly around the abandoned hospital. Around the corner: a group of girls with their pants pulled down and the smell of warm urine on cold cement. Laughing. She turned to vomit and soon felt a hand on her face.

Someone was gently moving the hair from her eyes. Someone was stroking her back. Horns sounded in her mind. An aura of light. *Not you,* is what she said to the petrol-station boy when she turned around to meet the owner of the gentle hands and saw the little tuft of hair on his chin. The pierced ears. He was wiping her face with his shirt and saying something in her ear and Liliana was standing beside them, looking like a dog that's just been kicked.

NOVEMBER

Icy draughts run through the corridors of the convent. Everything is bathed in cold blue light. In November, the sky turns black early in the afternoons. One morning, after prayer, the mother tells the nuns that the world too is dark. She makes bleak, obscure references to acts of violence. Dolores senses something apocalyptic. But the other nuns are expressionless, one of them yawns, and the mother won't elaborate except to say that certain events weigh heavy on the world. For these grave sins, she says, the nuns must suffer a little more. They will deprive themselves of any small pleasures. They will wake up, in the middle of the night, and pray for two hours.

At three in the morning, the bells ring. The nuns get up quickly and dress in the dark. They make their way to the chapel. The air is chilly. The room is murky purple from the light of the candles against the stained-glass windows. The nuns kneel in rows and, because of the cold, huddle their bodies together for warmth as they pray. Here is something new: bodies on either side of Dolores, trembling. Electricity in the room. Her lower back aches. The pain on her knees soon numbs. A warm feeling spreads across her lower half. She leans into the bodies. How long has it been? How long, how long? she thinks. Desire, what do the other nuns do with it?

She has heard that the bishop is due to return. Is all this excitement for him? His arrival is all anyone can talk about. This time, when he leaves the convent, he will take with him the three girls who are yet to take their vows. Hang Tooth, the moon-faced girl, and the beautiful one who bites her nails. They will leave early in the morning, before sunrise, wearing their ceremonial robes. And when the bishop returns with them to the convent in the early hours, the novices will be nuns. They will have new names.

Soon, the mother tells Dolores privately and plants a dry kiss on her forehead. The new girl is gone and Dolores is pet once more. In the study room, the mother takes her hands and holds them in her own. *Do-lor-es,* the mother whispers in her throaty voice, *the next seven months will pass quickly. Soon you will take your vows.*

For the first two weeks of November, at three in the morning when the bells ring, Dolores thinks about the letter she sent Liliana. She has calculated the time it would take for a letter to travel across the world and then back again. During morning prayers, she pictures Liliana opening the letter and crying. Or locking the letter, still sealed, in her childish wooden box. But something changes by the middle of the day. Dolores lets herself wonder if she might receive a reply. She even writes a letter to herself on behalf of Liliana, one that says all the things she wants to read. By the time the nuns sit down for dinner, Dolores has exhausted herself with worry and knows that Liliana will not write back. This is a trick. She is anticipating disappointment in order to protect herself. She knows that when the mother superior calls out names, she is still expecting to hear her own. But her name is never called, and the next morning, the whole process begins once more.

In the days before the bishop's arrival, the nuns wash the walls and floors of the convent with rags and hot water. They scrub the kitchen and the bathrooms with vinegar and bicarbonate of soda. They dust the chapel. In the middle of November, when the first snow falls, Dolores is vacuuming the study room, and she stops to watch it fall from the small window. It is the first time she has seen snow. She remembers blocks of hail falling from the sky when she was a child. Remembers holding her arms out to catch what her mother had then called snow.

Ever since she was young, Dolores knew that God could hear her thoughts. So, for her sanity, she created a private life, a space in her head that was impenetrable from the outside. Dolores learnt to follow through on an impulse so quickly that her mind didn't have time to catch up. There were the obvious temptations. Red emergency buttons. Wallpaper coming off a wall just waiting to be ripped. Then there was this. Sometimes, Dolores slapped herself hard on the face. She did it quickly and then continued with her day. Pure impulse, that's all it was.

This time, when the bishop comes to visit, he is a big red emergency button waiting to be pushed. Yes, the bishop, with his comb-over and his tinted glasses. His face like wet lettuce. The bishop, who repulsed her, with his strange little hands that shake. Just now, outside in the bright white snow, he walks with the mother superior. Dolores watches them from the study window. She is careful to keep sinful thoughts out of her head. Because since she has been living at the convent she feels the presence of God more intensely than she did before. So, she replaces the word *bishop* with *mountain*. She thinks: Look at that lovely, strong mountain in the distance. She thinks: What would it be like to wrap my body around that mountain? She thinks: If I were in the cradle of that mountain perhaps I would be safe.

She had never been on such a long flight. She had never travelled alone before. She had an envelope full of euros stuffed inside the front of her jeans. She was worried about the money, so she slept with her jeans on. Sitting next to her was an older couple with matching short grey hair. Sleek jackets. Big gold rings on their fingers. They asked Dolores questions. In their smiles was obvious bemusement. They told her they wanted to visit the Alhambra. Dolores nodded, even though she didn't know what it was. *I have a cousin in Seville,* she heard herself say in a voice that was not her own. Here is the thing: Dolores had no plan, even on the plane. When Dolores' mother convinced her father to let her visit – after her cousin's husband had offered to pay for her flight – this is what Dolores was thinking: in Spain, she would be as far away as one could possibly go. In another hemisphere, on the other side of the world.

Her cousin was waiting at the airport with a sign she had decorated with hearts and kisses. When she saw Dolores, she began to cry. She wasn't so bad, the cousin. She was half the size she had been since Dolores last saw her and her once long hair was cut into a dramatic bob. She had red puffy eyes. Even her mouth looked different. She used to pout. She used to lift her chin and talk to Dolores like she was a child. Now, in the car, her tongue was loose and she was talking fast. The cousin was driving with one hand and blowing her nose with the other. There were used tissues scattered all over the dashboard. Dolores rolled her window down and then up again. She was woozy from the heat. It had hit her as soon as they'd entered the car park. Now she felt it on her cheeks and at her neck. As they drove, her eyelids opened and closed and every now and then she caught bits of her cousin's monologue. *What does he expect?* the cousin was saying as she weaved in and out of lanes. She was talking about her husband. *Just selfish,* she was saying as she cut other drivers off with a half-hearted wave of her hand. They were passing flat fields of yellow grass. *I shouldn't be telling you this,* the cousin kept repeating. And then: *His mother. Yes, a conniving little woman.* Dolores closed her eyes and opened them once more. *Otherwise he is just limp,* said the cousin. And a little later: *I love him!*

Churches painted white and gold and mustard-yellow. Bells ringing. Blue-tiled walls. Archways, trams, and large palms. This was Seville. The heat began early in the morning and lasted long after the sun went down. Coiled-iron balconies and chandeliers in the bars. A park with a large pond and peacocks sauntering around.

On that first day in Seville, Dolores' cousin took her to the Basílica de la Macarena and they stood with the rest of the tourists holding their cameras high above the crowd, trying to get the best possible picture of the Virgin. Dolores had never seen anything so beautiful in her life – the Virgin – she wore a large crown on her head that fanned out like a peacock's feathers, only in gold. There were little spikes at the top of her crown in the shape of stars. Lace covered her hair. Four glass tears sat at the corners of her eyes and one frozen halfway down her cheek. Her eyebrows were creased. Her mouth slightly open. She was wearing plush robes in purple with gold trimmings and there was a fat emerald brooch pinned to the lace on her bust. *A gift,* Dolores' cousin whispered to her, *from a famous bullfighter.*

For the third time that day, the cousin began to cry. *Just look at her,* she was saying. She wiped the tears from her face and then solemnly placed her hands together, began to feverishly whisper Hail Marys. Dolores looked up at the Virgin once more and then at the room around her. It was dark and calm. Despite the crowd, the room was silent. She felt strange and she said so in her head. I feel so strange, she told herself.

Outside, the sun was blinding. There were three women standing by the exit. They had rotted teeth and pale gums and the oldest one was missing a leg. The three women were dressed in long black dresses and the youngest was dangling a screaming baby in one arm. *No,* the cousin said, sternly, and her hand went up like a stop sign as the legless one jangled a cup of loose change under their noses. Dolores felt something being pressed into her palm. It was a small red rose. She looked at the woman who had given it to her and then at her baby who was screaming. He had grey eyes and there was a thick trail of dried green snot around his nose. *Shoo,* said the cousin, flicking her hand twice. She turned to Dolores, *Let's eat?*

As they walked through the crowds, the cousin

told Dolores that her husband always made a big show of giving the women some coins to make himself feel better and that if there wasn't an audience around to watch she doubted he would even care. *He's such a phoney*, she said. As they walked, the streets became less crowded and the cousin directed them to a small bar opposite a church. There, the cousin ordered pork cheek and a carafe of red wine. She ate an olive, spat out the pit, tore some bread and stuffed it into her mouth, announcing loudly: *I'm going to get very drunk.* The wine arrived. They drank it quickly and without talking. (Why not, why not, why not? Dolores was thinking.) It was chilled and slightly sweet. The sky was blue and cloudless. They ate the pork cheek. It melted in Dolores' mouth. She thought about licking the plate. The cousin ordered more wine. *My love,* she yelled. The husband emerged from behind Dolores, began planting kisses on the cousin's head. He was short, with brown hair and blue eyes and slight stubble on his chin. A bright orange linen scarf was delicately arranged around his neck. Immediately, the cousin assumed a coquettish expression, lowering her chin and pouting her lips. *My love, my love, my love, we missed you, but you're late again! My sweet baby cousin comes to visit from halfway across the world and look what you do. What kind of gentleman are you? To keep two young and beautiful ladies waiting?* Here was the cousin Dolores remembered. *Hello,* the husband said, and as he leaned over to kiss Dolores on the cheek, the cousin fell off her stool.

The following week they took her to Córdoba. There was a heatwave. During the day, the three of them stayed in their hotel room with the air conditioning turned on. Because it was all that was available, they shared one room with two beds – a double for the cousin and her husband and a fold-out for Dolores. When the sun finally set, they went outside and walked around. The yellow light from the street lamps against the buildings and the cobbled streets made everything look as though it were in soft focus. Blurry. Almost otherworldly, this yellow glow.

They visited the Mezquita-Catedral. Inside, the room was expansive, with columns and half-moon arches in red and white – the mosque on one side and the cathedral on the other. At one end were Arabic inscriptions in gold. At the other, little ornate faces of cherubs adorned portraits of the Virgin. And as they passed each artefact, the husband whispered to Dolores and the cousin, saying this or that was Gothic or from the Renaissance or Romanesque. *Look,* he said, gesturing with his hand, *see how large this room is? It was designed so that the soul could wander around freely in order to converse with God.* The three of them stood in silence. A palpable awe filled the room. Everything was still. Serene.

The cousin turned to her husband and frowned. *Why aren't you wearing your nice scarf?*

At dinner that night they ate gazpacho, rabbit, and roast vegetables. They drank three carafes of red wine. The cousin pulled Dolores close and drunkenly slurred: *We're still newly-weds, we need time alone in the hotel.* Her husband, also drunk but in earshot, looked briefly horrified. Dolores excused herself and left the restaurant. It was almost midnight and the air outside was warm and heavy. She walked aimlessly, looking at families and babies in strollers and stray dogs chasing their tails. She heard the sound of horns and faint drumming in the distance. A procession, she thought, and followed the sound. As she walked, the streets became crowded. She turned a corner, elbowed her way to the front and there it was: a gold coffin covered in flowers and candles and raised high above her head, the sculpted body of Christ inside. She had never seen so many different shades of gold. She had never felt the sound of a horn penetrate her heart. Above her, confetti fell from the windows of apartments. Incense smoke billowed. All around her, people were crying. She bowed her head. The gold coffin passed before her eyes. Twelve sets of legs, just visible, shuffling underneath. The marching band followed. She looked up and kept her eyes on the procession until it turned into a glint of gold in the distance. Until the marching band was once again the faint sound of horns and drums. Until the crowd dispersed and she was suddenly alone on the street in the hot night air, standing next to a wilting palm.

When she returned to the hotel room, her cousin was sitting on the bed with a smug look on her face. She assumes I'm still a virgin, Dolores thought. The cousin's husband emerged from the bathroom and she told them both what she had seen. They put their shoes on and ran outside. Dolores sat on the bed alone in the harsh light of the hotel room. She could hear the rumbling of the air conditioner. Her body was covered in sweat. She could also hear, faintly, the sound of a baby crying. *I'm going mad*, she said, out loud. It was coming from the room next door. She turned on the television and turned up the volume to drown out the sound. Images flashed across the screen: a wide expansive desert, smoke billowing and red flames, the infamous black and white mushroom cloud above Hiroshima. Blurry footage of men wearing balaclavas and camouflage. She switched channels, pausing on the image of a woman with peroxide curls sitting in front of a screen that depicted a pixelated image of the Egyptian pyramids. The woman had a holy cross on her desk. Her eyes were heavily made-up and her lips were bright pink. She held tarot cards in her hands. A telephone number flashed at the top of the screen. Thirty euros for thirty minutes; fifty euros for an hour. Dolores took her cousin's credit card from the safe. She picked up the hotel phone and dialled. A sultry voice answered: *You are speaking with Rosa. Is it a matter of the heart or money troubles?* Dolores had barely heard the call ring. *Neither,* she managed to answer. She told the woman that what she needed was help. *My sweet child, don't you know you have an archangel protecting you? His name is Michael and he looks after the most helpless of us all. Is it revenge you seek?* Dolores tried to name her troubles. She stumbled over words. She spoke around things. At certain intervals, an automated voice interrupted to announce the minutes remaining. *For this, my sweetest angel, I must consult my cards.* The woman took her time. Dolores heard sharp breaths, and then a long, soft groan. *Ah, I see. Firstly, you need to understand that this is all part of His plan, I assure you. In one week, on the night of San Juan, light a candle, preferably pine, plait your hair in three places, blow out the candle and bury the wick.* In the hotel room, Dolores listened and felt her body sinking further into the bed. The woman continued talking. As Dolores went to hang up, she heard the automated voice cut in once more: *Press zero and then the hash key for an extra two minutes.*

DECEMBER

It's a crisp, dark morning when the bishop leaves with the three novices. Hang Tooth, the moon-faced sister, and the beautiful one who bites her nails. They are cloaked in special robes. A crown of thorns sits on each of their heads. All day, Dolores had watched them walking together in silence through the corridors and in the dining room while they ate. They no longer say her name. No more lingering on the middle syllable. They act like she doesn't exist at all. They are so close to being official. It's snowing when the mother unlocks the gates. Dolores gets up to watch from the window. The mother kisses each of their heads. The three of them sit in the back of the bishop's car. The bishop, now chauffeur, sits in the front and starts the engine. It splutters. He starts it once more. He inelegantly manoeuvres the car down the driveway and it disappears underneath the trees on the road that leads down the mountain.

They return that evening while everyone is in bed. Dolores hears the car in the driveway outside. Hears the groan of the gates. She pulls the blankets over her head so that her eyes are shielded. She hears their footsteps in the corridor. When the three enter the room, they go to their beds in silence. Dolores listens to their breath until she is sure they are asleep. During morning prayer in the chapel, she studies their faces. The way each of them moves. They wear new robes and a thick, starched veil. Yes, they have new names, but Dolores knows, she can tell, that nothing has changed. They are exactly the same.

The bishop is still hanging around the convent. He sniffs around the kitchen, sticking his fingers into freshly baked bread. He takes a spoon and tastes the soup. It dribbles down his chin. In the afternoons, he takes long naps in the study room. He hovers around the nuns while they do their chores. *Very good,* he whispers. *Something smells nice,* he says from the doorway of the kitchen. *God be with you,* he says whenever he leaves the room and he lazily makes the sign of the cross – his hand moving only slightly towards his head, his chest, left and then right. Dolores is aware of the power that must come with making such a half-hearted sign of the cross. And truly, it's his power that she craves. Why shouldn't she? In the convent, since June, she has been on the very lowest rung.

By now, Dolores has given up on the idea that she might receive a letter. Now, she winces in the evenings when the mail is handed out. It hurts to even think about that time of day. She refocuses all of her attention on the bishop. She refuses to think of anything else. Liliana, Angelo, the mess she has made, the strange drama unfolding inside her body.

At night, when everything is dark and the others are asleep, Dolores touches her face and her neck. Her breasts are swollen. Her stomach is bloated. She has nightmares in which her whole lower half bursts open. The bells interrupt the touching. She pulls her heavy body up. At one in the morning, the convent is unbearably cold. In the chapel, she huddles with the other nuns. At three, when they walk back to their rooms, Dolores lingers at the back of the line.

At the end of December, she realises that the bishop, like the mountain, has been in front of her, on the horizon, for some time now. When it happens, it's not the way she had imagined, though she knows now that things rarely unfold like they do in the dark, private theatre of her mind.

The bishop is walking through the garden. It's snowing. Dolores has gone to collect the eggs. As she walks inside the chicken pen, she knows that he is watching her. So, she lingers a while, thinking perhaps he will follow. She stands with her back resting against the wooden panels. There, amongst the cool, stale smell of shit and hay, holding eggs in both hands, she knows that she's never felt so ridiculous and so miserable in her life. The bishop enters. There is some talk: *Many eggs today. Yes, Father. God be with you,* et cetera, et cetera. In one clumsy movement, the bishop's tongue goes straight to her mouth. His shaking hands hover over her breasts and he kisses her neck. Her hands are around his body, turned upwards, holding the eggs. He kneels and his cold hands go under her smock, pulling down her two sets of stockings, her underwear. His saliva is warm. His tongue moves all over her legs in messy licks, going upwards, until it's inside her. Her whole lower half shakes. He moves his hands from her breasts to her stomach. Pure, hot panic runs through her. It's one of those impulse thoughts: Drop the eggs on his head, she thinks, and she does it quickly. The bishop looks up. His face is coated in thick streams of goo. Dolores pulls up her stockings and underwear, she runs.

Outside, the mother superior is standing in the snow. She looks at Dolores and then behind her, at the bishop, who is still kneeling on the ground, wiping his face.

That night, in bed, Dolores feels the usual rumbles in her stomach and at the bottom of her bowels. The rumbling enters her dreams. She wakes up to the sound of high-pitched squealing coming from the bed beside her. The rumbling is both inside and out. All around her the furniture moves. The earth trembles. Then, silence. Everything is still. *An earthquake,* says the moon-faced sister. The rest of the nuns fall to their knees. They pray. Dolores, sitting upright in bed, moves her arms so that they fall on either side of her body. They had been wrapped tightly around her belly.

It was the day before she was due to fly home. In Seville, she packed a small backpack with the things she thought she might need: clothes, money, toiletries, passport, rosary beads, and, for good luck, the small postcard she had bought of the Virgin of Macarena. She took her cousin's Bible too. It was one of five books that sat on an empty bookshelf in the corner of the living room among romance novels. When she left, it was the middle of siesta, and the cousin and husband were both in bed. She told them through the door that she wanted to go to the park and see the peacocks. They mumbled goodbye. Outside, the sun was blinding hot and everything was shut. She walked to the train station in the heat and bought her ticket. The man behind the counter wrote down instructions for her on a scrap of paper. Her train left at seven. She would need to change trains after midnight. In the morning, she would need to find a taxi or a bus to get up to the top of the mountain. At the station, Dolores sat in the bar in front of a fan and, because she didn't know what else to do, slowly drank three espressos. Then she went to the bathroom to empty her bowels. Inside the train carriage, everything was blue – the seats, the carpet, the row of curtains along the window, which everyone else in the carriage kept firmly shut. Dolores opened hers slightly. The sun was setting. Somewhere on the platform, the whistle blew. As she thought about getting off, the doors slammed shut. The train left the station. Her stomach began to turn. She closed her eyes and prayed. She took a dirty shirt from her backpack, balled it up into a makeshift pillow and put her head against it on the window. After a while, she fell asleep.

In the car, on the drive back from Córdoba, she had sat in the back seat looking out at the palm trees and the road signs that dotted the highway and quietly decided that she would not go home. Her cousin was in the front passenger seat, asleep. And as the husband drove, he spoke to Dolores about different vacations he had taken with his family when he was young. He told her about caves in Granada, about riding a ferry across blue waters to Tarifa, about an uninhabited island near Marseille with nothing on it but white rocks and wild flowers and an old, unused army base. He had seen so many things. He told her about visiting Pompeii and seeing those bodies calcified by volcanic ash, frozen in their moment of death. He described the shapes of the bodies – two lovers embracing, a mother covering her child – curved outlines of human figures holding their faces or hugging their knees. He remembered hiking through limestone mountains in the Basque Country, those high peaks that, over time, had formed into strange shapes from glacial movement. There was a convent somewhere in those mountains, he said, and during the night, lying in their tent, his family heard the bells of the convent ringing and the wind blowing and wolves howling and nothing else. And while the husband said all of this and more, Dolores was listening quietly in the back, asking him questions and catching his eye in the rear-view mirror. It was late and there were no other cars on the road and so they glided along the highway, the radio playing softly underneath the husband's voice – a whispering baritone, low and soothing. The air conditioning whirring. The road smooth and slightly bending. And Dolores felt safe, comfortable.

She wanted nothing more than to remain a passenger in this car driving along the highway, cloaked in the eerie calm of the night.

She woke abruptly to the sound of the train driver announcing her stop and pulled the blue curtain aside. It was just after midnight and the station was almost empty. Outside, the night air felt cooler than it had in Seville. She had an hour to wait until her next train. Next to the station, she found a small bar with brass trimmings and mirrored panels, lace tablecloths and hanging lamps. Rows of red vinyl booths. A woman sat on a stool behind the bar, her back hunched and her chin resting on her hands. Her eyes glued to a small television. Dolores took the corner booth. She counted the remaining coins in her purse, arranging them on the table in small towers.

A man wearing a brown leather jacket and sunglasses appeared on the other side of the window, his nose pressed up against the glass. *Hello,* he said. His smile revealed gold teeth. Dolores looked down. *Hey, hello?* he was saying, knocking on the glass. She pretended to count the coins in front of her. *Sweetheart, hello?* he said, and then he walked into the bar and sat opposite Dolores in the red vinyl booth.

Now, he said, *you're hungry? You should be hungry.* He clicked his fingers in the air. The woman behind the bar looked up, rolled her eyes, and then disappeared behind a door. After a while, she returned holding a plate of fried potatoes, which she slid onto their table without speaking. Steam was rising off the plate. The man began to eat. Red sauce dripped down his chin. He paused. *Eat,* he said. Dolores shook her head. *No, thank you,* she said. Her stomach gurgled. She was hungry. She looked out at the empty station. The man pushed the plate towards her. *Please,* he said. Dolores shook her head. She looked at the woman behind the bar. She tried to talk to her without using words. But the woman was hunched over, chin resting on hands, watching the screen in front of her. *Excuse me,* Dolores said. She picked up her bag and walked to the bathroom. Inside, she took one of the tablecloths that sat in a laundry basket and attached it to her hair with some pins from her purse. A makeshift veil. She took the Bible from her bag and held it in front of her. When she opened the bathroom door, the man looked up and frowned as she walked out.

There were only two other people sitting in her carriage on the next train. Dolores wrapped the straps of her backpack around her arms and fell asleep with her head resting on top. At one point, she woke and peeled the curtain open. The light hit her in the face. The sun seemed so close. That big, orange, fiery ball on the horizon turned everything outside gold. There was nothing green in sight. She closed the curtain and fell asleep once more. And when she woke later, she wondered if she'd dreamed it.

Her train arrived at seven and she spent the morning walking through the small town.

She saw a small hotel and a shop that sold hiking gear. One lonely restaurant. Nothing was open. An hour or so later, a bus pulled up beside her and she told the driver where she wanted to go. Inside, the bus was completely empty and it smelt like petrol. Dolores savoured the smell. She assumed a coquettish expression not unlike her cousin's when she told the driver that she had no money. She had on her veil and she was clutching the Bible. He looked her up and down and nodded. She sat up the front with her backpack on her lap. At first, they drove up the steep hill in silence. But when she caught his eye in the rear-view mirror, he looked away quickly and flicked the switch on his radio. It was an old pop song. Something she recognised from home. The road was curved. As they circled their way up the mountain, she looked out at the rocks and palms and wild shrubbery, the skeleton branches of burnt trees. On one of the hills, she saw what looked like thousands of small wooden crosses painted white. The bus abruptly stopped. The doors opened. As she got off, she asked the driver which way to walk. *God bless you, sister,* he mumbled, as he closed the doors.

JANUARY

After the earthquake, the mother superior decides that the nuns should fast. Breakfast is now a slice of bread, no butter. They skip lunch. Dinner is a small cup of soup (no bread). To drink water during the day, they must ask permission (*Try to drink only half a glass*, the mother says). They still pray between the hours of one and three in the morning but now, for a little more suffering, they go outside. It's January, and the air outside stings her uncovered skin. Dolores' hands and face go numb. Outside, in the middle of the night, holding a small torch, Dolores concentrates on the moon or the way that the light from the nuns' torches casts different shadows on the walls of the convent.

After the earthquake, inside the chapel, the mother superior had held Dolores' hands in hers and whispered: *What happened with the bishop was a test. An invitation to sin. Made by the Devil himself.* She encouraged Dolores to confess. To look upon the incident as an opportunity to strengthen her faith. In six months, the mother explained, Dolores would take her first vows. Now was the time to be saved. Dolores chewed on these words like tough meat. The earthquake had given her pause. She couldn't say with all certainty that it wasn't a sign. She believed in hell. She believed in the lure of the Devil, although not in the same way that the mother did. So, she censored her thoughts more rigorously. She no longer thought of leaving. She accepted that her fate – whatever that meant – was to be at the convent. And it felt like a large brick had been taken from her chest. She breathed more easily. Relief was light and airy. Like bouncing on little puffs of clouds. She walked the corridors of the convent with her head bowed. She got up at one in the morning, in a daze, and stood outside and prayed. She forgot about her mountain.

But a week or so after the earthquake, Dolores suddenly became absent from herself. She was tired all the time, she was clumsy. At dinner, she spilled soup down the front of her smock. While cleaning the bathroom, she took long whiffs of the disinfectant – as she usually did to savour the smell – then hit her head on the toilet bowl and blacked out. When she came to, she was woozy. During prayer, while kneeling in the chapel, she pinched herself to keep from falling asleep.

The night before it all unfolds, for the first time since she arrived at the convent, Dolores has a dreamless sleep.

It's one in the morning. She is standing outside in the snow. It feels as though a large balloon inside her body is expanding outwards and pushing down on her bladder. Something inside her somersaults and a wave of intense pain follows. She falls to her knees. The nuns are standing in a circle. Dolores prays. She asks for help. She makes all kinds of promises. *Anything*, she says out loud, *anything*. The mother is kneeling beside her. *My stomach*, Dolores says. She can see the lights from the torches dancing on the wall. Everything goes dark.

Images appear like strobe lights. Dolores is looking up at the stars. Her big body is inside a wheelbarrow. Fours nuns at the front and two at the back. They slowly push her down the long, sloped driveway. The convent bells are ringing non-stop. Halfway down the hill, they buckle and the wheel-barrow spins, Dolores comes flying out. Is this real?

Dolores thinks. *No,* she says out loud. She is now lying in the back seat of a car as it circles down the mountain. *Fahr schneller!* says a male voice in the front seat. *Ich versuch's doch! Es ist zu dunkel,* a woman replies. (Is that German? Dolores wonders.) On the floor of the car, Dolores can see hiking boots and poles, wet towels and a woollen rug. Warm water leaks out from inside her and dampens the seat. The pain at the bottom of her stomach returns.

The next thing Dolores is conscious of is a fat and hairy finger waggling back and forth. *You've been a very naughty nun, Dolores,* says the doctor. He has black oily hair and blue eyes. He chuckles, takes a pair of plastic gloves and pulls them over his hands. *May I, Sister?* he asks in mock earnestness, as he pulls up her hospital gown and sticks one of his fat fingers inside her. And in this moment, Dolores leaps into the dark. She tells the doctor she has never been in so much pain in her life. A gas mask covers her mouth. She inhales. The taste coats the back of her throat. It is sweet and slightly chemical. Dolores laughs. The lights go out.

She wakes and vomits. The pain arrives in monstrous waves. Time stops. Or rather, time becomes intervals of sweet release. She is squatting on the floor. Everyone around her is wearing blue. Paper masks around their mouths. Pink plastic gloves. She asks for her mother. I want my mother, Dolores thinks. *I want my mother,* she says out loud. They bring the mother superior into the room. Dolores groans. *Not her,* she says. They take the mother by the arm and lead her out. Hands help her back onto the bed. She looks at the light on the ceiling. She sees a tray of silver tools beside the bed, shimmering.

Voices whisper in her ears. *Sweetheart,* they're saying, *sweetheart.* She clenches her whole body. She goes in and out of pain. She concentrates on the eyes above the mask in front of her. Two wells of blue. The light on the ceiling begins to vibrate, turns into seven lights, seven small pools. She clenches her body and bites her tongue, tastes warm blood inside her mouth. She knows immediately when what was inside of her body is no longer there. She closes her eyes. When she opens them, she can hear the baby crying.

They put the baby on her chest. He is all red flesh. How can something so small make such a terrifying noise, Dolores thinks. His face is puffy and he has wet strands of black hair on his head. Mucus on his face. Large alien-like eyes that open and close. Little scrunched fists. Dolores watches his tiny chest swell up and deflate. Feels his warm and sticky body on her skin. What is this? she thinks. Her vision blurs. Two hands in pink gloves appear. They feel around the top of the baby's skull. Fingers poke inside his mouth. They pick the baby up and leave.

When she wakes again, she sees the mother superior and two of the other nuns. They're standing around the incubator beside the bed. *Francisco,* they're saying. *Francisco.* They pray. The mother turns to look at Dolores lying in bed. The smile falls from her face. Dolores closes her eyes and pretends to sleep. Later, she hears the mother talking to someone outside the room. *She's not a nun,* the mother says, *she is just someone we opened our doors to.*

Dolores opens her eyes. A squat, blonde nurse enters the room. She has a pouty mouth. *It's the celebrity nun,* the nurse says, and then something under her breath. Something ending with the words *immaculate conception.* The nurse smiles. She flicks the drip attached to Dolores' arm. She picks up the clipboard from the bottom of the bed. She is waiting for a response. She will not leave until she gets one. *My stomach hurt,* Dolores says. The nurse snorts.

They wheel Dolores into a different room. The

walls are yellow. A blue curtain surrounds the bed. She can't see the woman in the bed beside her but she can hear her talking to her baby. And she hears what the woman is watching on the television. Sinister music. An organ, some strings – a telenovela. The orchestra swells. The doctor with the oily hair returns. He examines her stiches. He murmurs to himself as he does. *Great. Fantastic. Very nice,* he says. Two nurses help Dolores into the shower. They wash and comb her long hair. They pat her dry and leave. Alone, in the harsh, cool light of the bathroom, for the first time in seven months, Dolores studies her reflection in the mirror. Her belly is bloated. Her breasts are swollen and her nipples are enormous. Her face is gaunt. She has large circles under her eyes. She barely recognises herself. She touches her hair, her face, her bony neck. She talks to herself, out loud, watching her lips move.

Outside the hospital, the air is crisp and the sun is bright. The car is black. The mother superior sits in the front, next to the driver, holding the baby. He is swaddled in a pale blue blanket. Two other nuns sit in the back. Dolores is wearing a clean dress, stockings, and a large brown jumper. The nurses help her out of the wheelchair and disappear back inside. Dolores is standing beside the car, motionless. *Dolores,* the mother says. *Get in.* Four sets of eyes look at her. Five, if you count the baby, whose eyes are now wide open, alert, and fixated on her own. *Dolores,* the mother repeats, *aren't you coming with us, child?*

ACKNOWLEDGEMENTS

Thank you to Seren Adams and Lettice Franklin.

Thank you to Amaryllis Gacioppo, Alena Lodkina, Madelaine Lucas, Harriet McKnight, Anthony Macris, Eleonora Naimo and Ryan Phelan.

Thank you to my family: John, Marie, Sacha and Tahira.